For Joe Douglas
*I.W.*

For Mum
*love David*

British Library Cataloguing in Publication Data
A catalogue record of this book is available from the British Library.

ISBN 0 340 79198 5 (HB)
ISBN 0 340 79199 3 (PB)

First published in 2001
by Hodder Children's Books,
a division of Hodder Headline Limited,
338 Euston Road, London NW1 3BH

10 9 8 7 6 5 4 3 2 1

Printed in Hong Kong

# All Change!

Written by Ian Whybrow

Illustrated by David Melling

Hodder
Children's
Books

A division of Hodder Headline Limited

It was the tiger's birthday
And he was quite upset.
Miss Lollipop said, 'There, there!
You're making me all wet.'
'I didn't get a present,'
The tearful tiger sighed.

Miss Lollipop said, 'Cheer up!
We'll go for a birthday ride!'

That was just what the tiger wanted
So they drove down a country lane.
Miss Lollipop shouted, 'All change!'
And they jumped aboard . . .

. . . a train.

They stopped at a seaside station
And picked up a billy goat.
The goat bleated, 'All change!'
So they jumped into ...

. . . a boat.

They rowed to where the seals live
And then put up the sail.
A seal barked, 'All change!'
And they jumped into . . .

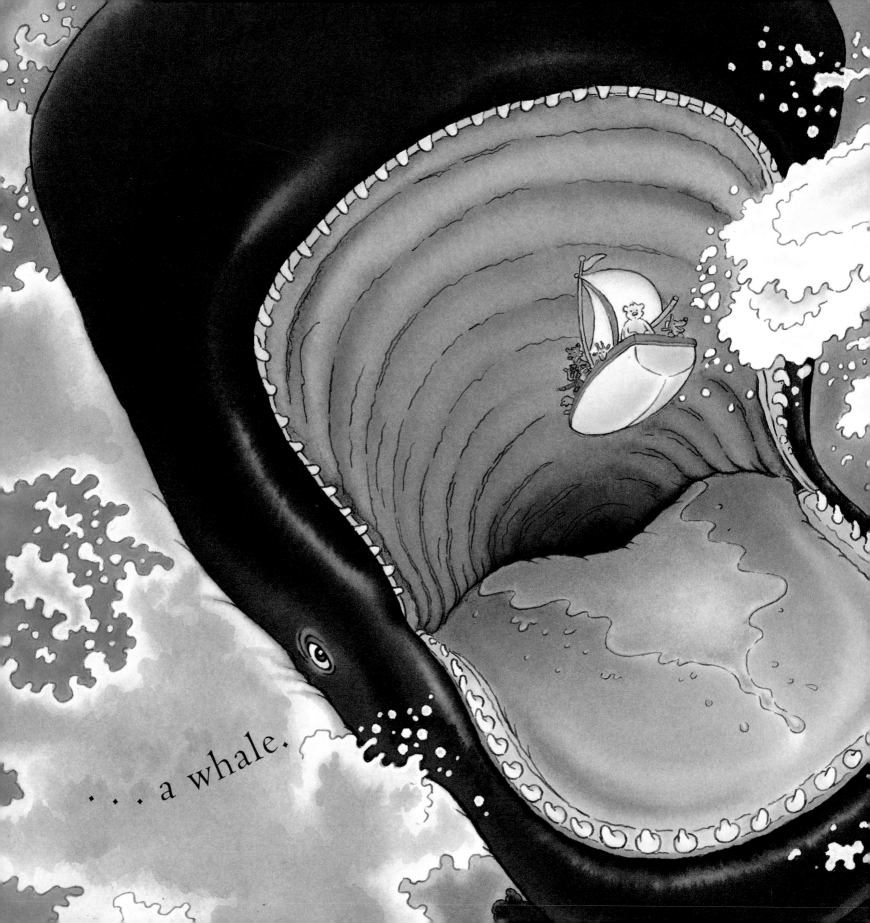

. . . a whale.

They rumbled in his tummy
And gave the whale a pain.
So he blew them all out through his spout
And they jumped into . . .

. . . a plane.

The plane flew high up in the sky.

Then they had a bit of luck.

The pilot shouted, 'All change!'
And they landed in . . .

. . . a dumper truck.

The dumper truck went bumpety bump
Which is just what animals like.
The puffin shouted,
'All change!'
And they jumped onto . . .

. . . a bike.

The bell on the bike went ding - aling - a - ling!
But they didn't get very far.
The tiger roared out, 'All change!'
And they jumped into . . .

. . . a racing car.

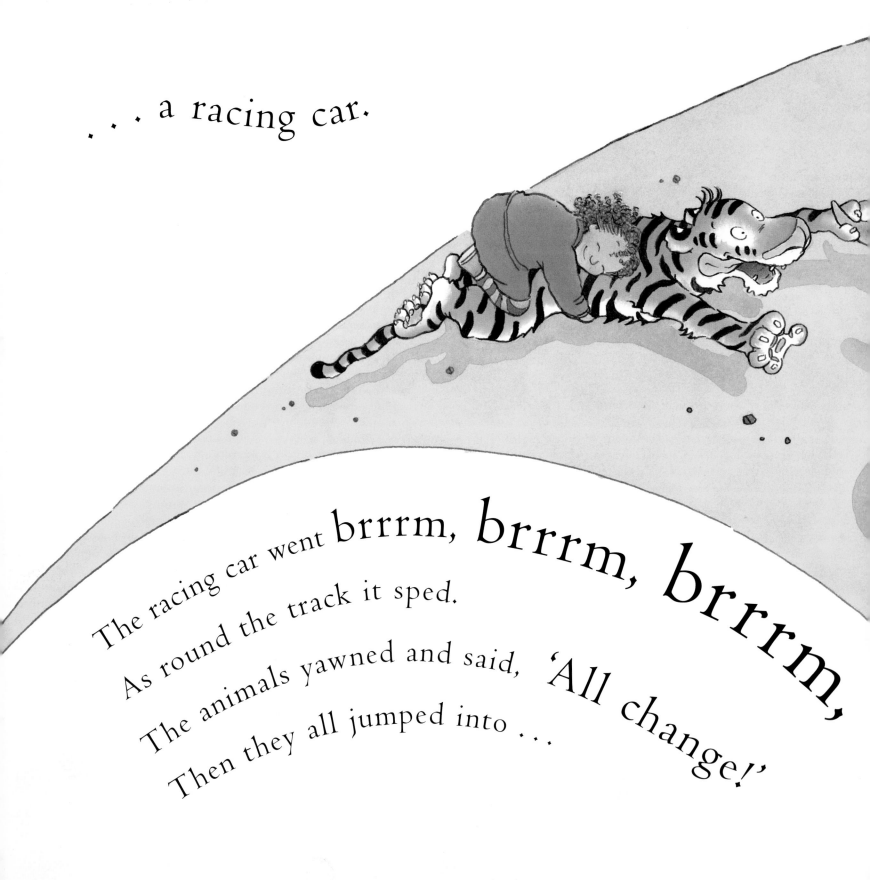

The racing car went brrrm, brrrm, brrrm,
As round the track it sped.
The animals yawned and said, 'All change!'
Then they all jumped into …

Wait a minute, wait a minute!
What did they change into?

Yes! They changed into their pyjamas!
But . . . wait a minute, wait a minute!
Then what did they do?

Yes! They helped the tiger open all his presents . . . and then they all had a piece of the tiger's birthday cake . . .

And at last the animals cleaned their teeth
and this is what they said:

'Night, night, Miss Lollipop!'
And they jumped into their · · ·

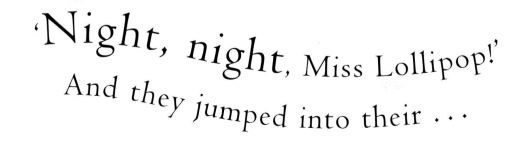

. . . bed!